THE CRIPPLED LAMB

To our special friends—
Kelly, Kasey, and Kara Wilson

ISBN 0-590-12246-0

Text copyright © 1994 by Max Lucado.
Illustrations copyright © 1994 by Liz Bonham.
All rights reserved. Published by Scholastic Inc., 555 Broadway, New York, NY 10012, by arrangement with Word Publishing.

12 11 10 9 8 7 6 5 4 3 2

Printed in the U.S.A.   14

First Scholastic printing, December 1996

THE CRIPPLED LAMB

by **Max Lucado**
with Jenna, Andrea and Sara Lucado
illustrated by **Liz Bonham**

SCHOLASTIC INC.
New York   Toronto   London   Auckland   Sydney

Once upon a time in a sunny valley, there lived a little lamb named Joshua. He was white with black spots, black feet, and . . . sad eyes.

Josh felt sad when he saw the other lambs with snow-white wool and no spots. He felt sad when he saw the other sheep with their moms and dads because he didn't have a mom or dad.

But he felt saddest when he saw the other lambs running and jumping, because he couldn't.

Josh had been born with one leg that didn't work right. He was crippled. He always limped when he walked.

That's why he always watched while the other lambs ran and played. Josh felt sad and alone—except when Abigail was around.

Abigail was Josh's best friend. She didn't look like a friend for a lamb. She was an old cow.

She was brown with white blotches that looked like rain puddles on a path. Her belly was as round as a barrel, and her voice was always kind and friendly.

Some of Josh's favorite hours were spent with Abigail.

They loved to pretend they were on adventures in distant lands. Josh liked to listen to Abigail tell stories about the stars.

They would spend hours on the hill, looking into the valley. They were good friends. But even with a friend like Abigail, Josh still got sad.

It made him sad to be the only lamb who could not run and jump and play in the grass.

That's when Abigail would turn to him and say, "Don't be sad, little Joshua. God has a special place for those who feel left out."

Josh wanted to believe her. But it was hard. Some days he just felt alone. He really felt alone the day the shepherds decided to take the lambs to the next valley where there was more grass. The sheep had been in this valley so long, the ground was nearly bare.

All the sheep were excited when the shepherd told them they were going to a new meadow.

As they prepared to leave, Josh hobbled over and took his place on the edge of the group.

But the others started laughing at him.

"You're too slow to go all the way to the next valley."

"Go back, Slowpoke. We'll never get there if we have to wait on you!"

"Go back, Joshua."

That's when Josh looked up and saw the shepherd standing
in front of him. "They are right, my little Joshua. You better
go back. This trip is too long for you. Go and spend the night
in the stable."

Josh looked at the man for a long time. Then he turned
slowly and began limping away.

When Josh got to the top of the hill, he looked down and saw all the other sheep headed toward the green grass. Never before had he felt so left out. A big tear slipped out of his eye, rolled down his nose, and fell on a rock.

Just then he heard Abigail behind him. And Abigail said what she always said when Josh felt sad. "Don't be sad, little Joshua. God has a special place for those who feel left out."

Slowly the two friends turned and walked to the stable together.

By the time they got to the little barn, the sun was setting like a big orange ball. Josh and Abigail went inside and began to eat some hay out of the feed box.

They were very hungry, and the hay tasted good.

For a little while, Joshua forgot that he had been left behind.

"Go to sleep, little friend," Abigail said after they finished eating. "You've had a hard day."

Josh was tired. So he lay down in the corner on some straw and closed his eyes. He felt Abigail lie down beside him, and he was glad to have Abigail as a friend.

Soon Josh was asleep. At first, he slept soundly,
curled up against Abigail's back. In his sleep he dreamed.
He dreamed of running and jumping just like the other sheep.
He dreamed of long walks with Abigail through the valley.
He dreamed of being in a place where he never felt left out.
Suddenly strange noises woke him up.

"Abigail," he whispered, "wake up. I'm scared."

Abigail lifted her big head and looked around.

The stable was dark except for a small lamp hanging on the wall. "Somebody is in here," Josh whispered.

They looked across the dimly lighted stable. There, lying on some fresh hay in the feed box, was a baby. A young woman was resting on a big pile of hay beside the feed box.

Joshua looked at Abigail, thinking his friend could tell him what was going on. But Abigail was just as surprised as Josh.

Josh looked again at the woman and the child, then limped across the stable. He stopped next to the mother and looked into the baby's face. The baby was crying. He was cold. The woman picked up the baby and put him on the hay next to her.

Josh looked around the stable for something to keep the baby warm. Usually there were blankets. But not tonight. The shepherds had taken them on their trip across the valley.

Then Josh remembered his own soft, warm wool.
Timidly, he walked over and curled up close to the baby.
"Thank you, little lamb," the baby's mother said softly.
Soon the little child stopped crying and went back to sleep.
About that time, a man entered the stable carrying some rags.
"I'm sorry, Mary," he explained. "This is all the cover I could find."
"It's okay," she answered. "This little lamb has kept the new king warm."
A king? Joshua looked at the baby
and wondered who he might be.
"His name is Jesus." Mary spoke
as if she knew Josh's question.
"God's Son. He came from
heaven to teach us about God."

Just then there was another noise at the door. It was the shepherds—
the ones who had left Joshua behind. Their eyes were big, and they
were excited.

"We saw a bright light and heard the angels . . ." they began.

Then they saw Joshua next to the baby. "Joshua! Do you know
who this baby is?"

"He does now." It was the young mother who was speaking.
She looked at Joshua and smiled. "God has heard your prayers,
little lamb. This little baby is the answer."

Joshua looked down at the baby. Somehow he knew this was a special child, and this was a special moment.

He also understood why he had been born with a crippled leg. Had he been like the other sheep, he would have been in the valley. But since he was different, he was in the stable, among the first to welcome Jesus into the world.

He turned and walked back to Abigail and took his place beside his friend. "You were right," he told her. "God does have a special place for me."

ANGELICA, ISLAND PRINCESS

by Lara Bergen
based on the screenplay by Kate Boutilier
illustrated by Larissa Marantz and Shannon Bergman

Simon Spotlight/Nickelodeon

New York   London   Toronto   Sydney   Singapore

Based on the TV series *Rugrats*® created by Arlene Klasky, Gabor Csupo, and
Paul Germain, and *The Wild Thornberrys*® created by Klasky Csupo Inc., as seen on Nickelodeon®

SIMON SPOTLIGHT
An imprint of Simon & Schuster Children's Publishing Division
1230 Avenue of the Americas, New York, NY 10020
Copyright © 2003 Paramount Pictures and Viacom International Inc.
All rights reserved. NICKELODEON, *Rugrats*, *The Wild Thornberrys*,
and all related titles, logos, and characters are trademarks of Viacom International Inc.
All rights reserved, including the right of reproduction in whole or in part in any form.
SIMON SPOTLIGHT and colophon are registered trademarks of Simon & Schuster.
Manufactured in the United States of America

2 4 6 8 10 9 7 5 3

ISBN 0-689-85450-1

"Listen up, babies," said Angelica, clutching her doll, Cynthia. "Uncle Stu ruined our fancy cruise vacation and he's in big trouble! It's 'cause of him we're gonna hafta live here forever."

"All we gots to do is go into the topical drain forest and find Nigel Strawberry. He can help us get home!" said Tommy. "Come on, guys!"

Tommy and the other babies started off into the rain forest in search of Nigel Thornberry. Tommy was sure the TV star was somewhere on the island filming one of his nature specials.

"Hey! You babies hafta stay here and start being my royal subjects!" Angelica shouted after them. "I'm warning you! Giant mutant lobsters are gonna eat you with a side of butter! Now get back here!"

Angelica couldn't stand being ignored. "I gots to find someone to be my royal subject," she told her doll as she stomped along the beach. "There's gotta be someone around here I can boss. . . ."

Suddenly she heard a chimp chattering.

"Like a monkey, for example," she said.

Angelica crept up to a pile of rocks and peered around them. She could hardly believe her eyes. A teenage girl was having her toenails painted by a chimp dressed in a tank top. Angelica had found Debbie Thornberry!

"Listen up, monkey," Debbie was saying. "All that chimp chatter really bugs me. Just hand over those Cheese Munchies and keep painting."

"Wow," whispered Angelica. "She's got that monkey waiting on her hoof and mouth. I could learn a lot from that girl!"

"Excuse me, Miss Bossy Lady?" Angelica called out.

"Who's calling me a lady? I'm a teen!" Debbie replied. Then she saw Angelica. "Where did you come from?" she asked, jumping out of her seat. "This is supposed to be a deserted island."

"I'm Angeli-tiki, the island princess. And I'm thirsty," said Angelica as she plopped down in Debbie's chair and finished off her soda. "I lost my touch for being bossy, so you gotta teach me."

Debbie scanned the messy campsite, and then smiled sweetly at Angelica.

"Okay then," said Debbie, grabbing her headphones. "Stack the dishes, pick up the garbage, and clear the table."

Angelica looked at the mess and had a better idea. "Can I get you another soda first, Miss Teen Lady?" she asked. "'Cause you look extra-thirsty."

"Sure, thanks," Debbie replied. "Extra ice, two straws."

As Angelica headed into the Commvee, Debbie chuckled to herself and said, "I'd trade her for a monkey any day."

"Angeli-tiki is nobody's slackey," Angelica muttered to her doll. "We gotta get out of here, Cynthia."

She wandered to the back of the Commvee and spied a little trap door in the floor. Debbie poked her head in just as Angelica was peering down into the hatch.

"Hey . . . what's that bubble thing?" Angelica asked her.

"A bathysphere," Debbie replied. "It goes underwater, like a submarine. It's a blast to drive and—hey, quit stalling. Get my soda and get cleaning!"

"Sheesh. That girl's even bossier than me!" said Angelica as she returned to her snooping.

Angelica picked up a pair of binoculars and looked out the window just as the babies came toddling into view. They were headed up the side of a volcano!

"Those dumb babies are practically on top of that mountain and I'm gonna get blamed!" exclaimed Angelica. She was supposed to be watching them, after all. "I gotta go home and pretend I'm innocent."

Angelica threw open the
Commvee door and called to
Debbie. "I just 'membered . . .
I'm supposed to be home
for . . . uh . . . the island
sacrifice."

"My mom will drive you as
soon as she gets back," Debbie
assured her.

"But I have to go now!" Angelica
cried. "I'm the princess."

"Oh, okay," said Debbie as
they climbed into the Commvee.

Debbie steered the Commvee along the beach. Just then Spike burst out of the rain forest followed by Eliza Thornberry and Darwin! Debbie quickly swerved to miss them—and skidded into the surf. Luckily she pulled the BOAT MODE lever just in time.

"Debbie!" called Eliza, out of breath, "There's a bunch of babies lost around here, and there's a leopard after them!"

Angelica quickly unbuckled her seat belt. "If Drooly loses a piece of ear, I'm gonna be in big trouble!" she said to herself.

Then she dashed toward the back of the Commvee, yanked open the bathysphere hatch, and jumped in.

"I gotta get out of here! C'mon, Cynthia," she said to her doll. "We're taking a ride in the bathie thing."

Panicking, she tugged on the first lever she could find and—WHOOSH! The bathysphere dived beneath the ocean waves . . .

. . . and popped up again on the shore of an underground lake.

"Adoy, babies!" she exclaimed as she popped open the top hatch and waved at Tommy and his friends. "Look what I got. C'mon in . . . keep it moving. We don't have all day."

Tommy was leading an unfamiliar grown-up to the door.

"Who's that?" Angelica asked.

"Nigel Strawberry," Tommy declared.

"That's your TV hero?" Angelica said in disbelief. He looked like a giant baby!

Angelica sat back down and stared at the bathysphere's controls. Then she pretended to drive while Susie looked on.

"This scrubmarine hasn't moved a bit, Angelica," she complained.

"Carmichael, nobody likes a backstreet driver," retorted Angelica. She reached out and yanked a lever.

ZOW! SPLASH! WHOOSH! Off zoomed the bathysphere, landing with a thud on the ocean floor.

Nigel Thornberry was thrown against the wall and knocked out when the bathysphere hit bottom.

"Oh, no! Nigel Strawberry!" yelled Tommy, rushing over to him. "This calls for my 'mergency bottle." With that, he pulled a bottle from his diaper and squirted milk in Nigel's face.

"Oh, hello there," said Nigel, blinking at the babies. "Who are all you positively adorable children?"

"We're shipwrecked and we want to go home!" cried Susie.

"Well, of course you do, young lady. And so we shall," replied Nigel.

Luckily Debbie and her mom, Marianne, got through to the bathysphere's radio at that very moment. "We're coming to get you, Nigel. Is everybody okay down there?"

"Excellent, dearest!" said Nigel. "Here we go, children! Won't be long now. . . ."

When the bathysphere finally resurfaced, Angelica popped open the hatch and ran into the arms of her parents.

"Princess!" they crooned.

Angelica smiled. Nothing gets you out of trouble faster than nearly being lost at sea!

"Nice driving, Angeli-tiki!" said Debbie, winking.

"Thanks, bossy teen lady!" replied Angelica. "Now," she said quietly, "if I could just get those stinky babies to start listening to me again. . . ."